Let's Make a
JOYFUL
NOISE

Written by **Karma Wilson**

Illustrated by **Amy June Bates**

zonder**kidz**

ZONDERVAN.COM/
AUTHOR**TRACKER**

www.zonderkidz.com

Let's Make a Joyful Noise!
Copyright © 2008 by Karma Wilson
Illustrations © 2008 by Amy June Bates

Requests for information should be addressed to:
Grand Rapids, Michigan 49530

Library of Congress Cataloging-in-Publication Data
Wilson, Karma.
    Let's make a joyful noise! : a celebration of Psalm 100 / by Karma
Wilson.
       p. cm.
    Illustrated by Amy June Bates.
    ISBN-13: 978-0-310-71119-3 (jacketed hardcover)
    ISBN-10: 0-310-71119-3 (jacketed hardcover)
    1. Bible. O.T. Psalms C–Paraphrases, English–Juvenile literature.
I. Bates, Amy June, ill.. II. Title.
BS1450100th .W55 2008
242'.62–dc22

2005036219

Published in association with Writer's House, LLC

Editor: Bruce Nuffer
Art Direction and Design: Laura Maitner-Mason

Illustrations used in this book were created using watercolors.
The body text for this book is set in Century Old Style.

Printed in China

08 09 10 11 12 • 10 9 8 7 6 5 4 3 2 1

To Pastor Steve Robins–
who makes the most joyful
"noises" I've ever heard
— K.W.

For my Mom and Dad
— A.B.

Celebrating Scripture Psalm 100:1
Make a joyful noise unto the LORD, all ye lands. (KJV)

Let's make a joyful
noise to the LORD!

ding-do[r]

tweet-a-tw... tweet

The birds all sing, and the church bells ring.
The birds seem to sing as loud as they can.
The church bells ring, and I want to sing
And make a joyful noise to the LORD!

Tweet-a-Tweet Tweet
Ding Dong Ding

Let's make a joyful noise
to the LORD!

A guitar starts strumming, the choir is humming,
and I want to hum as loud as I can!
The guitar is strumming, and I am humming,
and I make a joyful noise to the LORD!

Strum, Strum, Strum
Hum, Hum, Hum
Tweet-a-Tweet Tweet
Ding Dong Ding

Let's make a joyful noise to the LORD!

The people clap, and my foot starts to tap,
and I want to tap as loud as I can!
The people clap, and I want to tap
and make a joyful noise to the LORD!

Let's make a
joyful noise to the LORD!

The piano plays, and we all sing praise,
and I sing praise just as loud as I can!
The piano plays, and we all sing praise
and make a joyful noise to the LORD!

Hallelujah!
Hallelujah!
Clap, Clap, Clap
Tap, Tap, Tap
Strum, Strum, Strum
Hum, Hum, Hum
Tweet-a-Tweet Tweet
Ding Dong Ding

Let's make a joyful
noise to the LORD!

hallelujah!

hallelujah!

hall

Birds are singing, bells are ringing.
The guitar's strumming, the choir's humming.
People are clapping, feet are tapping.
The piano plays, and we sing our praise.

We sing about angels high up above us.
We sing about heaven and all the joy there.
We sing about Jesus and how much he loves us.
We sing about God and his wonderful care!

Hallelujah!
Hallelujah!
Clap, Clap, Clap
Tap, Tap, Tap
Strum, Strum, Strum
Hum, Hum, Hum
Tweet-a-Tweet Tweet
Ding Dong Ding

We make a joyful noise to the LORD!
A joyful noise to the LORD!

It's so much fun, and then when we're done.
We all bow our heads and quietly pray,
we ask God to guide us and be there inside us.
And I thank the LORD for this great, noisy day.

And my prayer is a joyful noise to the LORD.
A very joyful noise to the LORD.

Amen!